P9-CLR-189

Henry and Mudge

AND THE

Snowman Plan

Story by Cynthia Rylant

Pictures by Suçie Stevenson

SCHOLASTIC INC.

New York Toronto London Auckland Sydney
Mexico City New Delhi Hong Kong Buenos Aires

For Samantha J. Wills—CR

For Benjamin Brown especially, and also for Joshua and
Dennis Brown, and for Amy van der Clock Brown—SS

No part of this publication may be reproduced in whole or in part,
or stored in a retrieval system, or transmitted in any form or by any means,
electronic, mechanical, photocopying, recording, or otherwise,
without written permission of the publisher.
For information regarding permission, write to Simon & Schuster Books
for Young Readers, Simon & Schuster Children's Publishing Division,
1230 Avenue of the Americas, New York, NY 10020.

ISBN 0-590-04083-9

Text copyright © 1999 by Cynthia Rylant.
Illustrations copyright © 1999 by Suçie Stevenson. All rights reserved.
Published by Scholastic Inc., 557 Broadway, New York, NY 10012,
by arrangement with Simon & Schuster Books for Young Readers,
Simon & Schuster Children's Publishing Division.
SCHOLASTIC and associated logos are trademarks and/or
registered trademarks of Scholastic Inc.

20 19 18 17 16   11 12/0

Printed in the U.S.A.   40

First Scholastic printing, November 2002

The text of this book is set in 18-point Goudy.
The illustrations are rendered in pen-and-ink and watercolor.

Contents

Contest!

On a snowy day in January,
Henry and Henry's big dog Mudge
saw a sign in a store window.
It said SNOWMAN CONTEST,
SATURDAY AT THE PARK.

"A snowman contest!"
said Henry. "Wow!"
Mudge wagged his tail.
He always wagged his tail
when Henry said, "Wow."
It meant excitement.

And sometimes it meant
dessert!
Henry ran home
to tell his father.

Henry's father was in the
basement, painting a chair.
He had green paint on his
hair, across his nose,
and in his mustache.

"Guess what, Dad?" said Henry.

(Mudge was looking for a

special old boot.)

"What?" asked Henry's father.

He wiped some paint across his chin.

"There's a snowman contest on
Saturday!" said Henry.
"Snowman contest!" said Henry's
father. He wiped some paint
on his ears. "Wow!"

"Can we go?" asked Henry.

"Sure!" said Henry's father.

He wiped some paint on his
elbow.

Henry looked at his father.

Henry looked at the chair.

"Dad, I think that chair has been
painting *you*," said Henry.

Henry's dad looked at himself
in an old mirror.
He had green hair, a green nose,
a green mustache, a green chin,
green ears, and a green elbow.
Henry's dad looked at Henry.
He said, "You should see me
when I paint a *house*!"

At the Park

On Saturday, Henry and
Henry's father and
Henry's big dog Mudge
went to the park.
There were many people there.

All of the people had things.

They had shovels and spoons.

They had hats and shoes.

They had rocks and carrots
and marbles and broccoli.
"*Broccoli?*" said Henry
to his father.

And, of course, they all had dogs.

"It looks more like a

wagging contest to me,"

said Henry's father.

Mudge wagged and wagged.

Henry and his dad had already
made their snowman plan.
They looked at each other.
They shook hands.
"Good luck, break a leg,
and don't let the bedbugs bite,"
said Henry's father.
And they got to work.

While Henry and his father built
their snowman, Mudge visited.
He visited a poodle.

He visited a husky.

He visited a dachshund
who didn't want to visit him.

Then he found a carrot to
chew on.
A Chihuahua helped him chew it.
Mudge finished his half first.

It looked like the Chihuahua
might finish hers
sometime in July.
Mudge wagged and
gave her a kiss.

Snow Aliens

By 3:00 all of the snowmen
were ready for the judges.
Henry and his father
looked around the park.

There were snowpeople.

There were snowcats.

There were snowdogs.

There were snow aliens.

And one person had built
a snow Abraham Lincoln.
"Wow!" said Henry.

The judges walked all around.

Henry was feeling nervous.
He held Mudge's collar.
Holding Mudge's collar
always helped when
Henry was nervous.

"I hope they like ours,"
Henry said.
"Me too," said Henry's dad,
holding Mudge's collar
on the other side.

Finally the judges arrived.
They looked carefully at the
snowman Henry and his father
had built.
They looked at the front.
They looked at the back.
They looked all around.

Finally one of them asked,
"What is it?"
"It's my dad when he's painting
a chair," said Henry.

The judges looked again
and laughed and laughed.
Mudge wagged and drooled
on their boots.

When the winners were
announced, first place went
to Abraham Lincoln.
Second place went to a
snow leopard.

And third place went to
the snowman with paint
in his mustache.
"Yay!" yelled Henry.
Henry and Henry's father
proudly looked at their prizes.

One was a purple ribbon.

It said THIRD PLACE WINNER,

MOST ORIGINAL SNOWMAN.

And the other prize was

a big box of snowman cookies.

"I sure am glad you're a
messy painter, Dad,"
said Henry.
"I'm an even messier *eater*,"
said Henry's father.

And he and Henry
and Henry's big dog Mudge
took their prizes home and
made a wonderful cookie mess.